Frizzy Haired ZUZU

BY MEDEIA SHARIF
ILLUSTRATED BY BASMA HOSAM

Magination Press • Washington, DC • American Psychological Association

To my mom, for her
infinite amounts of inspiration—MS

To Oday my husband, partner, and home.
To Emma my everything—BH

Books for Kids From the
American Psychological Association

Text copyright © 2023 by Medeia Sharif. Illustrations copyright © 2023 by Basma Hosam. All rights reserved. Except as permitted under the United States Copyright Act of 1976, no part of this publication may be reproduced or distributed in any form or by any means, or stored in a database or retrieval system, without the prior written permission of the publisher.

Magination Press is a registered trademark of the American Psychological Association.
Order books at maginationpress.org, or call 1-800-374-2721.

Book design by Christina Gaugler

Printed by Lake Book Manufacturing LLC, Melrose Park, IL

Library of Congress Cataloging-in-Publication Data
Names: Sharif, Medeia, 1976- author. | Hosam, Basma, illustrator.
Title: Frizzy Haired Zuzu / by Medeia Sharif; illustrated by Basma Hosam.
Description: Washington, DC : Magination Press, [2023] |
Summary: When Zuzu straightens her curly hair, everyone thinks she looks fantastic, but Zuzu does not feel like herself without her frizz, and decides to keep her beautiful hair just the way it is.
Identifiers: LCCN 2022057333 (print) | LCCN 2022057334 (ebook)
ISBN 9781433841576 (hardcover) | ISBN 9781433841583 (ebook)
Subjects: CYAC: Self-acceptance—Fiction. | Hair—Fiction. |
Kurds—Fiction. | LCGFT: Picture books.
Classification: LCC PZ7.S52975 Fr 2023 (print) | LCC PZ7.S52975 (ebook) | DDC [E]—dc23
LC record available at https://lccn.loc.gov/2022057333
LC ebook record available at https://lccn.loc.gov/2022057334

Manufactured in the United States of America

10 9 8 7 6 5 4 3 2 1

Zuzu has an amazing puff of curly red hair.
But that's not all there is about her...

Zuzu loves riding her bicycle and dancing to all types of music.

She swings her arms and twirls around. Her frizzy curls bounce as she dances.

But she hates her hair. The older she has gotten, the bigger it has grown.

Other children tease her about her *mezin* hair.

Her sister, Gulistan, offers to help.

"Let's flatten it!" she says.

They don't have a flat iron, but Gulistan finds a curling iron. "Maybe it'll reverse my curls," Zuzu says.

But reversing the curls only makes them bigger.

She massages a cup of sesame oil into Zuzu's hair.

But the oil makes her hair too delicious.

Then, her mother offers to help.

"How about I try brushing?" her mother says.

Zuzu fills with hope as her mother tugs and pulls her hair with a brush.

Berivan gasps.

Gulistan puts her hand over her mouth.

Her mother becomes pale.

"Give me a mirror!" Zuzu demands.

Her hair is even
BIGGER!

She gathers all her allowance money and all the money she received from her grandparents for her last birthday. She runs out of the house.

Zuzu bikes to the nearest hair salon.
She had never been to one before.

Zuzu bursts into tears. "Straighten my hair, please!"

"*Insh'Allah*, I will fix your hair," one of the stylists says.

The hairstylist shampoos and conditions. She dries. She uses a flat iron. Steam rises from Zuzu's hair.

Zuzu is afraid to look in the mirror. She holds her breath, and then she releases it. She is amazed by what she sees. Her hair becomes straighter and straighter.

Zuzu isn't sure if she likes her hair like this. It's so different. Her straight hair is shiny but not as soft as her bouncy curls. She doesn't look or feel like her usual self.

Zuzu rides home.

"Is that Zuzu? Your hair is different... so flat. No puff, no curl, and no bounce! Keça jwan."

She makes a face at her friends. Their compliments make her wonder about what's beautiful to them, to her...

It starts to rain. Music pours from the open window of a neighbor's house. Instead of going inside, Zuzu dances. She knows what the rain will do to her hair, and it's what she wants.

Zuzu dances and dances with her friends. Her curls bounce around her head and shoulders. Her puff of curly red hair comes back. She finally feels like herself again.

GLOSSARY

insh'Allah – if God wills (Arabic)

keça jwan  – pretty girl (Kurdish)

mezin [mah-zahn] – big (Kurdish)

READER'S NOTE

I wrote this book because I've had frizzy hair my whole life. "Frizzy" is a term used to refer to hair that's dry in texture. Instead of staying in defined waves or curls, the strands stray in different directions. When I was young and didn't understand my hair texture, I would brush it in a way that made it puffier. Currently, my frizz is in full force during humid times, but not as bad or non-existent when the weather is dry.

I pretty much tried everything Zuzu has done to tame my frizz and curls. I've used numerous gels, mousses, brushes, flatirons...you name it, and I've tried it. My hair journey, and my journey writing this book, has made me realize that hair can be a sensitive topic, especially if it's the type of hair that doesn't fit the norm. Frizzy hair is genetic, meaning that it's passed on from one generation to another, and some people in my family have hair like Zuzu's. My mom's tales from her Iraqi Kurdish childhood inspired me to write this book. From my mom's time to today's time, frizzy hair touches on social and emotional issues including diversity, boundaries, and self-confidence. A few reminders:

- One of the awesome things about being people is that we have variety. Embrace diversity since beauty comes in all forms.

- As adults, we should be mindful of how we talk about our own hair and other people's hair. If we say things like, "I hate my frizz," or "That girl should straighten her hair," we're revealing our attitudes about appearance. Children pick up on these messages and might follow our train of thinking

by conforming to the idea that non-frizzy hair is the best hair. There's no one type of hair that's best. All types of hair are beautiful. Notice in a positive way how we're all unique. Model an attitude of joy about how different we all are.

- Everyone's hair is different. People have given me one suggestion after another for my hair. Some things worked for the short-term, some things didn't work at all, and some things even damaged my hair badly. Just because certain routines or products are effective for one person's hair, it doesn't mean they're right for everyone else.

- Model healthy boundaries. However it's intended, it's not okay for people to comment on another person's appearance. If someone is criticizing your hair or "helpfully" offering suggestions that make you uncomfortable, you can say something like, "I like my hair this way," or "I know you're trying to help, but I don't wish to discuss my appearance with you."

Own who you are, no matter what type of hair you have or what kind of hair day you're experiencing. Likewise, celebrate your child's inner qualities and remind them that they're more than their hair. They're able to go about their day accomplishing so much—like riding their bike, dancing, being a good friend, doing their homework, and working toward their goals—no matter what their hair looks like. Like Zuzu, they and their hair are both glorious.

Medeia Sharif received her master's degree in psychology from Florida Atlantic University. She is a public school teacher and the author of *Remembering Mom's Kubbat Halab*. She lives in Miami, Florida. Visit medeiasharif.com and @medeiasharif on Instagram.

Basma Hosam graduated from the Faculty of Fine Arts in Cairo. She has illustrated over 30 books, including *Al Anatekh Kingdom* which received the Etisalat Award for Arabic Children's Literature in 2022. She has worked with Oxford University for an Arabic language project and is also the author-illustrator of *Something Searching for Himself*. She lives in Cairo, Egypt.

Magination Press is the children's book imprint of the American Psychological Association. APA works to advance psychology as a science and profession and as a means of promoting health and human welfare. Magination Press books reach young readers and their parents and caregivers to make navigating life's challenges a little easier. It's the combined power of psychology and literature that makes a Magination Press book special. Visit maginationpress.org and @MaginationPress on Facebook, Twitter, Instagram, and Pinterest.